Fartste

Kathleen Krull and Paul Brewer

Illustrated by Boris Kulikov

Simon & Schuster Books for Young Readers
New York   London   Toronto   Sydney

To our nephew Cyrus Mayer, another talented performer—K. K. and P. B.

To Mira, Eugene, Anna, and Liza Shats—B. K.

Acknowledgments

Rubin Pfeffer, Alyssa Eisner Henkin, Susan Cohen, David Gale, Navah Wolfe, Gery Greer and Bob Ruddick, Gerry Fialka, those who have cheered us on with this idea over the years. —K. K. and P. B.

SIMON & SCHUSTER BOOKS FOR YOUNG READERS
An imprint of Simon & Schuster Children's Publishing Division
1230 Avenue of the Americas, New York, New York 10020
Text copyright © 2008 by Kathleen Krull and Paul Brewer
Illustrations copyright © 2008 by Boris Kulikov
SIMON & SCHUSTER BOOKS FOR YOUNG READERS is a trademark of Simon & Schuster, Inc.
Book design by Daniel Roode
The text for this book is set in Garamond.
The illustrations for this book are rendered in mixed media
(acrylic, goache, watercolor, ink) on Fabriano paper.
Manufactured in China
2 4 6 8 10 9 7 5 3 1
CIP data for this book is available from the Library of Congress.
ISBN-13: 978-1-4169-2828-7
ISBN-10: 1-4169-2828-6

"I tell you, we are here on Earth to fart around,
and don't let anybody tell you different."
—Kurt Vonnegut (1922–2007)

Joseph Pujol was a French boy of eight
When he stumbled upon his very best trait,
While splashing around in the ocean one day
Not far from his house in the town of Marseille.

One minute, by chance, he was flexing his gut.
The next, he had sounds coming out of his butt!
Joe gasped with the shock, then roared with delight,
And soon he was sucking in air day and night.

High or low, soft or loud, and sweet, even tart—
He was honing his skill: the art of the fart.
Noise from his backside—wow, what a gift!
His fartistic training was amazingly swift.

In the army his buddies would fall on the floor
As he squeezed out some songs—or the loud sounds of war.
They'd all laugh so hard at the music they'd hear
From Private Pujol, who was playing his rear.

Joseph grew up to become a fine baker—
Of tarts and baguettes, a respectable maker.
He married Elizabeth, had a family of ten,
And put on a show for his kids now and then.

With so many Pujols, money was tight.
He tried to pay bills by performing at night.
Everyone laughed when he dressed as a clown,
Played the trombone, or sang around town. . . .

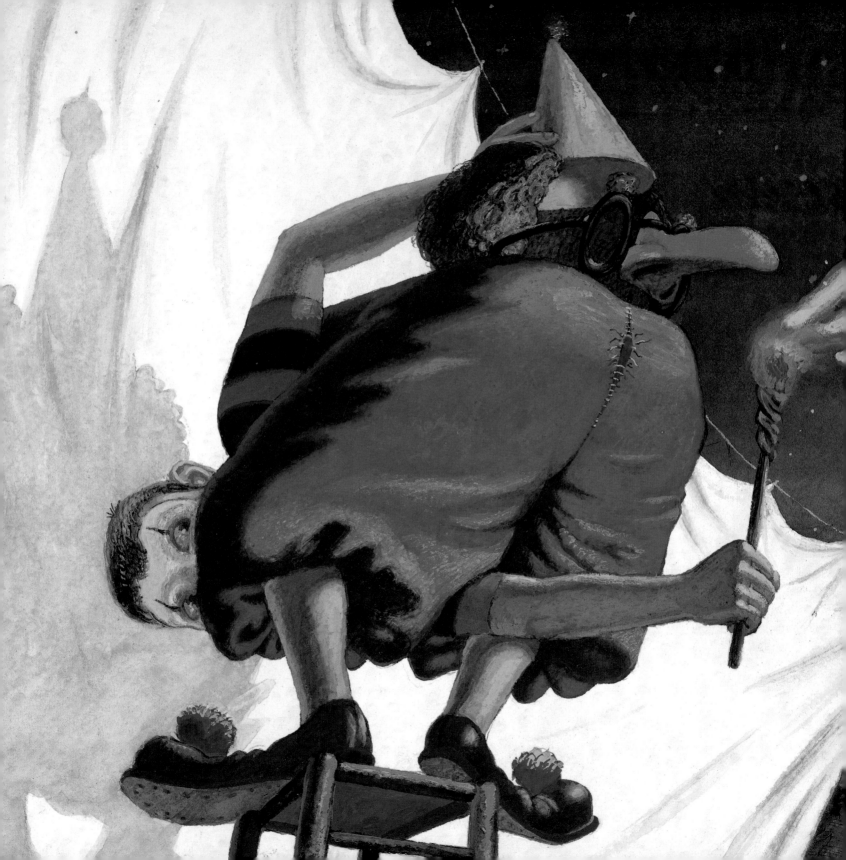

At long last he used a skill no one had:
In public, on stage, he farted. Egad!
Fashioning music out of the air,
Blasting out tunes from his own derriere.

One day a baker with butter and yeast,
And the next—*voila!*—he was JOE, *the Fartiste.*

Joe made his way to the great Moulin Rouge,
In the city of Paris, at a hall that was huge.
There Sarah Bernhardt, who was all the rage,
Earned eight thousand francs every night on the stage.

Dancers kicked wildly to light up the hall,
And Toulouse-Lautrec was painting it all.
The city was shining, a grand place for a show—
But was Paris ready for farts from our Joe?

Up on the stage was this tall dashing guy—
Long red coat with tails, white shirt and a tie.
His black satin pants had a very strange shape,
With a hole in the back for the air to escape.

Solemn and calm, not a sign of stage fright,
Joe fired off noises most impolite.
Announcing a sound, with a face oh so serious,
Performing it straightway—Mysterious! Delirious!

He could whisper or sneeze: *achoo!* gesundheit!
Or *boom boom*—blast off like a gun or dynamite.
Animal sounds he'd do, like an "arf!" from a dog,
A cry from a rooster, a "croak" from a frog.

A bit of Beethoven, a song by Mozart,
A Debussy ditty—all through a fart.
Men chewed their mustaches, keeping straight faces,
While women went breathless, in corsets with laces.

As Joe carried on, there were snickers and wiggles,
Followed by a chorus of uncontrollable giggles.
Finally shrieks of mirth would be heard.
Could you die laughing? He was just so absurd!

Nurses were stationed in the aisles to scout
For those laughing so hard they completely passed out.
Joe never stopped adding new sounds to his act,
Keeping the theater completely jam-packed.

The strangest part of his story to tell
Is that his flatulent actions completely lacked smell.
With air in him for seconds, no problem at all—
No hint of a scent that would stink up the hall.

Presidents came, even a king and a queen,
Raising their brows, wanting to deem him obscene.
But no matter how proper or sophisticated,
All of them ended up discombobulated.

He led sing-alongs, for convulsions of froth
Increased when he sounded the r-r-r-ripping of cloth.
He'd blow out the gaslights on stage, one by one,
To bid people adieu, then *poof*—he was done.

Famous and loved, the Fartiste at his height
Was pulling in twenty thousand francs every night.
The toast of Paree from January to December,
Those who saw him will forever remember:

Of all the performers (maybe last but not least),
Was the man who made his pants dance: JOE, *the Fartiste*.

Encore

*"I can truthfully say that I have never seen {people} laugh, cry,
shout and scream as they did when this little man with his . . .
deadpan face pretended to be unaware of his incongruities.
People were literally writhing about. Women, stuffed in their corsets,
were being carried out by nurses. . . ."*
—Eyewitness at a Moulin Rouge performance of *Le Petomane*, 1895

Yes, Joseph Pujol was a real person, born in Marseille, France,
in 1857.

One summer day when he was eight, he was with his family
at the beach. While exploring the ocean floor, he held his
breath. Suddenly he felt a blast of water *inside* his stomach area.
He rushed to shore and watched a stream of salt water flow out
of himself. At first he was horrified, thinking this was some

dreadful disorder. But soon he realized he had the ability to control the muscles of his intestines. With a great deal of practice, he was able to take air into his sphincter and release it in a wide variety of sounds.

He became a baker, but he earned extra money by performing. In Marseille, he launched *Le Petomane*—a polite variation of the French *peteur*, one in the habit of farting. The title meant something like "Fartomaniac." In English it is often translated as the "Fartiste."

Hardly anyone showed up at his first performance. After the giggles spread through town, the hall he rented above the train tunnel was full every night. Pujol's goal was to take his act to Paris. Artists, poets, and composers roamed the city, making it the cultural capital of the world. One artist, Henri de Toulouse-Lautrec, painted posters of the wild cancan dancers at the most famous theater of all: the Moulin Rouge (French for "Red Mill"). In a circuslike atmosphere, the legendary hall hosted singers and actors, only the best of the best. Sarah Bernhardt, the greatest actor of her day, was one of its biggest draws.

In 1892, at age thirty-five, Pujol arrived in Paris, where the Moulin Rouge immediately hired him. On the day of his first performance, he gazed at the famous giant windmill, lit up with newfangled electric lights, atop the hall. "What a marvelous fan for my act," he joked. That night, in the garden area known as the Elephant, he shared space with an enormous wooden elephant.

In turn-of-the-century France—with no TV, radio, or movies—he was instantly famous. A performer who made farting his entire act! He was purely funny, with no political message whatsoever. All levels of Victorian society dissolved into helpless laughter. King Leopold II of Belgium made a point of seeing the show. The Austrian psychiatrist Sigmund Freud kept a portrait of Pujol in his office and spoke of his influence (probably on his theories about anal fixation). The American inventor Thomas Edison filmed a few precious seconds of the show for the Paris Exhibition of 1900. French composer Erik Satie, piano player at the Black Cat Bar, was a prankster under

Le Petomane's spell. Pujol hung out in cafés with the Spanish artist Pablo Picasso and other painters, the influential playwright Alfred Jarry, and Toulouse-Lautrec himself.

Pujol was able to keep going for years, moving his family into a fancy chalet. He remained devoted to his children, some of whom went on stage as mime artists and magicians. But after 1918, World War I made the sound of gunfire all too real. Four of his beloved sons went off to fight, two of them coming home disabled. He lost his heart for performing. In his old age Pujol allowed doctors to examine his body, reporting in medical journals about his muscles and digestive process. He died in 1945 at the age of eighty-eight, surrounded by fond grandchildren.